# At the Bakery

Dona Herweck Rice

**Publishing Credits**

Rachelle Cracchiolo, M.S.Ed., *Publisher*
Conni Medina, M.A.Ed., *Managing Editor*
Nika Fabienke, Ed.D., *Content Director*
Véronique Bos, *Creative Director*
Shaun N. Bernadou, *Art Director*
Valerie Morales, *Associate Editor*
John Leach, *Assistant Editor*
Courtney Roberson, *Senior Graphic Designer*

**Image Credits:** All images from iStock and/or Shutterstock.

**Library of Congress Cataloging-in-Publication Data**

Names: Rice, Dona, author.
Title: At the bakery / Dona Herweck Rice.
Description: Huntington Beach, CA : Teacher Created Materials, [2019] | Audience: K to grade 3. |
Identifiers: LCCN 2018029692 (print) | LCCN 2018034557 (ebook) | ISBN 9781493899074 | ISBN 9781493898336
Subjects: LCSH: Baking--Juvenile literature. | Cupcakes--Juvenile literature. | Cookies--Juvenile literature. | Bakeries--Juvenile literature. | Brownies (Cooking)
Classification: LCC TX763 (ebook) | LCC TX763 .R48 2019 (print) | DDC 641.81/5--dc23
LC record available at https://lccn.loc.gov/2018029692

**Teacher Created Materials**
5301 Oceanus Drive
Huntington Beach, CA 92649-1030
www.tcmpub.com

**ISBN 978-1-4938-9833-6**



Printed in China
WaiMan

She would like to

make a  .

cupcake

She would like to

make a  .

pie

She would like to

make a  .

cookie

She would like to

make a  .

brownie

She would like to

make a  .

cake

She would like to

make a  .

doughnut

She would like to

make a  .

cinnamon roll

She would like to

make a  .

muffin

She would like to

make a  .

pretzel

She would like to

make a  .

loaf

# High-Frequency Words

## New Words

like make
she would

## Review Words

a to